Teggs is no ordinary dinosaur –
he's an **ASTROSAUR!** Captain of
the amazing spaceship DSS *Sauropod*,
he goes on dangerous missions and
fights evil – along with his faithful
crew, Gipsy, Arx and Iggy.

For more astro-fun visit the website
www.astrosaurs.co.uk

Read all the adventures of
Teggs, Gipsy, Arx and Iggy!

RIDDLE OF THE RAPTORS
THE HATCHING HORROR
THE SEAS OF DOOM
THE MIND-SWAP MENACE
THE SKIES OF FEAR
THE SPACE GHOSTS
DAY OF THE DINO-DROIDS
THE TERROR-BIRD TRAP
THE STAR PIRATES
THE CLAWS OF CHRISTMAS
THE SUN-SNATCHERS
REVENGE OF THE FANG
THE CARNIVORE CURSE
THE DREAMS OF DREAD
THE ROBOT RAIDERS
THE TWIST OF TIME
THE SABRE-TOOTH SECRET

Read the full set of Astrosaurs Academy adventures!

DESTINATION DANGER!
CONTEST CARNAGE!
TERROR UNDERGROUND!
JUNGLE HORROR!
DEADLY DRAMA!
CHRISTMAS CRISIS!
VOLCANO INVADERS!
SPACE KIDNAP!

Find out more at www.astrosaurs.co.uk

Astrosaurs

THE SABRE-TOOTH SECRET

Steve Cole

Illustrated by Woody Fox

RED FOX

THE SABRE-TOOTH SECRET
A RED FOX BOOK 978 1 862 30551 9

Published in Great Britain by Red Fox,
an imprint of Random House Children's Publishers UK
A Random House Group Company

First Red Fox edition published 2011

7 9 10 8 6

Text copyright © Steve Cole, 2011
Cover illustration and cards copyright © Dynamo Design, 2011
Map © Charlie Fowkes, 2011
Illustrations by Woody Fox, 2010
© Random House Children's Books, 2011

Typeset in Bembo MT Schoolbook by Palimpsest Book Production Limited,
Polmont, Stirlingshire

Red Fox Books are published by Random House Children's Publishers UK,
61–63 Uxbridge Road, London W5 5SA

www.randomhousechildrens.co.uk
www.randomhouse.co.uk

Addresses for companies within The Random House Group Limited can
be found at: www.randomhouse.co.uk/offices.htm

THE RANDOM HOUSE GROUP Limited Reg. No. 954009

A CIP catalogue record for this book is available from the British Library.

Penguin Random House is committed to a sustainable future for
our business, our readers and our planet. This book is made from
Forest Stewardship Council® certified paper.

MIX
Paper from
responsible sources
FSC® C018179

Printed and bound in Great Britain by Clays Ltd, St Ives plc

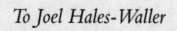

To Joel Hales-Waller

WARNING!

THINK YOU KNOW ABOUT DINOSAURS?

THINK AGAIN!

The dinosaurs ...

Big, stupid, lumbering reptiles. Right?

All they did was eat, sleep and roar a bit. Right?

Died out millions of years ago when a big meteor struck the Earth. Right?

Wrong!

The dinosaurs weren't stupid. They may have had small brains, but they used them well. They had big thoughts and big dreams.

By the time the meteor hit, the last dinosaurs had already left Earth for ever. Some breeds had discovered how to travel through space as early as the Triassic period, and were already enjoying a new life among the stars. No one has found evidence of dinosaur technology yet. But the first fossil bones were only unearthed in 1822, and new finds are being made all the time.

The proof is out there, buried in the ground.

And the dinosaurs live on, way out in space, even now. They've settled down in a place they call the Jurassic Quadrant and over the last sixty-five million years they've gone on evolving.

The dinosaurs we'll be meeting are

 part of a special group called the Dinosaur Space Service. Their job is to explore space, to go on exciting missions and to fight evil and protect the innocent!

These heroic herbivores are not just dinosaurs.

They are *astrosaurs*!

NOTE: The following story has been translated from secret Dinosaur Space Service records. Earthling dinosaur names are used throughout, although some changes have been made for easy reading. There's even a guide to help you pronounce the dinosaur names on the next page.

Talking Dinosaur!

How to say the prehistoric
names in this book . . .

STEGOSAURUS - *STEG-oh-SORE-us*

IGUANODON - *ig-WA-noh-don*

TRICERATOPS - *try-SERRA-tops*

HADROSAUR - *HAD-roh-sore*

DIMORPHODON - *die-MORF-oh-don*

APATOSAURUS - *a-PAT-oh-SORE-us*

DRYPTOSAURUS - *DRIP-toh-SORE-us*

PTEROSAUR - *teh-roh-SORE*

THE CREW OF THE
DSS SAUROPOD

**CAPTAIN
TEGGS STEGOSAUR**

ARX ORANO,
FIRST OFFICER

GIPSY SAURINE,
COMMUNICATIONS
OFFICER

IGGY TOOTH,
CHIEF ENGINEER

Jurassic Quadrant

Ankylos

Steggos

Diplox

INDEPENDE
DINOSAUR
ALLIANCE

vegetarian

sector

Squawk
Major

Outpost Q

PTEROSAURIA

DSS
UNION OF
PLANETS

Tri System

Corytho Lambeos

Iguanos

Aqua Minor

Geldos Cluster

Teerex
Major

Olympus

TYRANNOSAUR
TERRITORIES

carnivore
sector

Raptos

Planet Sixty

THEROPOD EMPIRE

Cryptos

Megalos

vegmeat
zone
(neutral space)

EA REPTILE
SPACE

Pliosaur
Nurseries

Not to scale

THE
SABRE-TOOTH
SECRET

Chapter One

MISSION TO OUTPOST Q

"There it is," said Captain Teggs Stegosaur. "Outpost Q, the secret space-observation station – and we've got to guard it!"

Teggs was an eight-ton, orange-brown stegosaurus. He had a reputation for bravery, daring and pie-eating unrivalled throughout the galaxy. His spaceship, the DSS *Sauropod*, was the

1

finest in the Dinosaur Space Service, and his best friends – Iggy, Arx and Gipsy – were the coolest crew members he could ever hope to have.

And yet, as he looked at Outpost Q on the *Sauropod*'s scanner screen, he had a strange feeling of foreboding. The station itself seemed unremarkable, like a steel box in space with a shining cylinder sticking out of the top. But Teggs felt a

tingling in his spiky tail that spoke of danger and death-defying adventure ahead.

"I don't get it," grumbled Iggy the iguanodon, the *Sauropod*'s chief engineer. "We're top-class, extra-tough astrosaurs. Why are we being sent to look after some mouldy old telescope?"

"It's a super-amazing *Mega*scope," Arx corrected him; the wise green triceratops

was Teggs's super-scientific second-in-command. "That thing is a million times stronger than any telescope, and a billion times more valuable. Carnivore war-planets won't like the way we can spy on them from the other side of space. They might try to steal its secrets."

"Or destroy it," said Gipsy, the high-powered stripy hadrosaur in charge of the ship's communications. "Is that all Outpost Q is then – a spy satellite?"

"It's much more than that," Arx explained. "It was built here at the edge of the Jurassic Quadrant to give the DSS early warning of any dangers from outer space – menacing meteors, approaching comets, even alien invaders."

"I hope it doesn't pick up too many of those," said Teggs, chomping on the lush ferns that grew

inside his control pit. "Not before I've
had my breakfast, anyway!"

Gipsy smiled – the
captain was on his
twelfth breakfast
already, and it
was only nine
o'clock in
the morning.
Suddenly, her
communicator
beeped. "Video
message incoming
from Outpost Q,"
she reported. "It's Chief Spotter Speck."

Arx's horns waggled with excitement.
"Speck is the Megascope's creator, a real
genius. I can't wait to see him!"

Teggs smiled. "Let's show him on the
scanner then."

Gipsy whistled to Sprite the
dimorphodon, leader of the *Sauropod*'s
flight crew of daring dino-birds.

He swooped down from a perch and hit the scanner switch with his beak. At once the image of Speck – a yellow, slightly podgy apatosaurus – filled the screen.

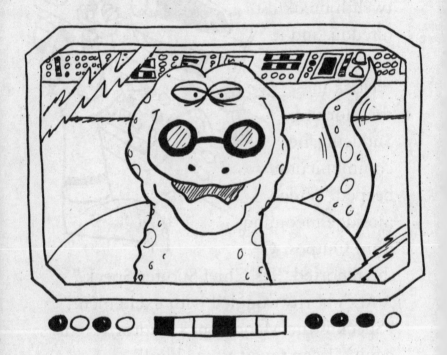

"Welcome, astrosaurs," said Speck, though he sounded more grumpy than friendly. "Thank you for coming to guard my outpost – though there really was no need."

"The DSS disagree," Teggs told him. "Remember, a triceratops scout ship spotted an unidentified flying saucer in this part of space a few days back. The saucer streaked away before the triceratops could challenge it, but they reported it was covered in weapons – and heading straight for you."

"Preposterous!" Speck spluttered. "I would've spotted such a ship through my Megascope."

"It might have camouflaged itself and sneaked past," Arx said gravely. "Now you've managed to make your invention so much stronger, Outpost Q has become a top target for enemy attack."

Teggs nodded. "The DSS is building a mega-strong defence system to protect you – force fields, pursuit probes, the lot. It'll be ready in a few days. Until then, we will patrol this area in case that flying saucer shows up again – and attacks."

"Sounds like a lot of fuss about nothing," said Iggy bluntly. "I still don't see what makes this Megascope so super-special."

Speck smiled. "How is your knee? I saw you bump it as you came aboard the *Sauropod*."

"What?" Iggy frowned. "How could you know that? No one was around, and we were on Tri Major – half the Vegetarian Sector away."

"That's no distance for my Megascope!" said Speck. "I've been following your progress since you left Tri Major so I knew when to expect you!" He sighed. "Oh, well. I suppose you won't go away until you've come on board Outpost Q to see my invention for yourselves ..."

"Wa-hooo!" Arx shot across to the lifts so fast that Teggs's ferns rustled in the breeze.

Teggs grinned. "We're on our way, Chief Spotter Speck. Over and out!"

Chapter Two

THE LIGHTNING-BOLT LEGEND

The dimorphodon flew the *Sauropod*
to Outpost Q, and within half an hour
the astrosaurs were safely on board the
space-observation station.

"Wow," said Gipsy, looking down
a huge white corridor. "This place is
enormous!"

"The crew of Outpost Q are all
apatosaurus," said Teggs, and Speck
lumbered over to greet them. "They're
huge. They need the extra room or they
would get stuck every time they got out
of bed!"

"Ah, there you are," said Speck, who
still seemed grumpy. "I can only give you

a brief tour, I'm afraid. We have a lot of space to study here – we can't afford *any* delays."

"Pardon us for being alive," Iggy muttered as he, Teggs, Arx and Gipsy followed the big yellow leaf-eater.

"First stop on our tour is the Data Room," said Speck. He opened a massive door to reveal hundreds of computers whirring away in a gleaming white chamber. An apatosaurus was checking

the screens and making notes on a digital clipboard.

"Oooh!" Arx cooed. "I suppose everything you spot through the Megascope is recorded, sorted and filed away here."

"Correct," said Speck.

"And yet you never spotted this mysterious flying saucer on your doorstep?" asked Teggs.

"Certainly not." Speck shook his head. "I believe it was nothing more than a smudge on that triceratops ship's scanner screen." He turned and strode away down the corridor. "Now, on your left you will see the entrance to the Star Chart Library – but I'm afraid we can't go in at this time."

Teggs saw a big sign on the door – LIBRARY CLOSED FOR CLEANING.

Arx looked longingly at the door, but Teggs nudged him along with his tail as Speck led the astrosaurs up a staircase to the next level.

"Now," said the Chief Spotter, "you are about to see Outpost Q's control centre – and the Megascope itself!"

As Teggs sprang up the steps, a sliding silver door opened to reveal the largest control room he had ever seen. The huge square walls and domed ceiling were thick glass, and through them Teggs could see the mind-boggling, mile-long Megascope jutting out into silent, star-spangled space.

Arx's jaw dropped in awe as he entered the room, and even Iggy seemed impressed. Gipsy marvelled at the busy instrument panels stretching right round the room, while Teggs watched the three apatosaurus carefully working the Megascope.

"It must take a lot of skill to operate

one of these," he remarked.

Speck puffed up his chest. "The real skill was in creating the Megascope. It works by magnifying starlight with giant galactic mirrors—"

"And passing it through a special space-lens to see halfway across the universe," Arx concluded, bubbling with enthusiasm. "No other dinosaur has worked out how to make the lens so strong. How did you do it, Chief Spotter Speck?"

"That's top secret, I'm afraid," said Speck.

Suddenly, one of the Megascope's operators jumped up. "Sir!" she spluttered. "The scope's spotted something. Something amazing!"

"Really?" Speck galloped over to join her, the astrosaurs at his heels. "What is it, Jodril?"

"I . . . I don't know how to tell you." Jodril was light blue, with enormous eyes

16

and thick fluttering lashes. It was clear she could hardly contain her excitement. "I've spotted a spaceship!" she gabbled. "A very old, very battered spaceship . . ."

Speck peered at the controls. "It's a long way out – about fifty trillion miles beyond the Jurassic Quadrant." He pressed a button and a faint lumpy image appeared on the screen beside him.

"It must be an alien craft," said Arx.

Iggy peered at the picture. "It looks to me like an old Dungmaster One. That's a dinosaur design – a real antique."

"And look, there's a name on the side," said Jodril.

Gipsy nodded. "It says . . . *Lightning Bolt*."

"*Lightning Bolt?*" Speck looked like he'd just been struck by one. "Are you certain?"

"That's the *Lightning Bolt* all right," Teggs murmured, a little shaken. "It belonged to the Jurassic Explorers – that brave band of dinosaurs who mapped out space in the early days of the Star-Dino Empire. They've always been my heroes."

"I remember reading about the *Lightning Bolt*," said Arx. "It went missing

18

without explanation three hundred years ago, never to be seen again."

"Until now," breathed Jodril.

"The last message it ever sent mentioned fanged monsters, terrible weapons and big trouble," Teggs recalled with a chill. "But space static cut the signal short. Rescue parties went looking, but the ship was never found."

Iggy whistled. "Must be a right old wreck by now. Drifting in space."

"But that's just it," cried Jodril. "It's moving too fast to be drifting – and in a dead straight line. The *Lightning Bolt* is being steered on a set course."

"That means there's somebody on board," Teggs realized. "But who?"

"I don't suppose we'll ever know," said Speck briskly.

"We certainly will," Teggs declared. "Because the astrosaurs will investigate!"

Speck frowned. "Are you sure that's wise?"

"That ship is a valuable piece of history," Teggs insisted. "We can't just let it disappear."

"Especially if someone really *is* on board," said Gipsy. "They could be the great-great-great-grandchildren of the Jurassic Explorers."

"Or else they're thieves who have stolen the *Lightning Bolt*," said Arx.

Iggy bunched his fists. "If they are, we'll soon sort them out."

"I must protest." Speck glared at the astrosaurs. "You were sent to guard Outpost Q!"

"He didn't want us here a few minutes ago," Gipsy muttered.

Teggs nodded thoughtfully. First a strange, unknown vessel had been detected near the Megascope – and now

the Megascope had spotted a legendary
spaceship.

Could the two events be linked
somehow?

"All right, here's the plan," said Teggs.
"Arx, you stay here on Outpost Q with a
team of ankylosaur security guards. Iggy,
Gipsy, you come with me in the *Sauropod*.
We will intercept the *Lightning Bolt* and
find out who or what is on board."

Arx saluted, Jodril beamed and Speck
grumbled under his breath.

"See you soon." Teggs turned and ran
from the room, racing back to his ship.
"The *Lightning Bolt* may have been away
for three hundred years, but I don't aim
to waste a single second in getting it
back!"

Chapter Three

THE SNARLING UNKNOWN

Teggs sent Alass, the tough ankylosaur leader of the *Sauropod*'s security crew, to help Arx guard Outpost Q – along with ten more ankylosaur guards, twenty dimorphodon to use as flying sentries, and three of the ship's six shuttles to patrol local space.

The astrosaurs held their farewell briefing in Outpost Q's docking bay.

"Travelling at top speed, it should take us a day to reach the *Lightning Bolt*," Iggy told Teggs.

"And another to bring it back with us," Teggs realized.

"We'll keep the outpost well-guarded

until then," Arx said confidently.

"Too right we will!" boomed Alass, thwacking her tail against the floor and startling several dimorphodon into flight. "Er, sorry."

"We'll keep an eye on you through the Megascope," said Jodril.

"And as soon as you've brought that ship back, I'd like you off my observation station," said Speck briskly. "I can't afford so many silly delays."

"I'll miss you too, Chief Spotter," said Teggs with a straight face.

"The *Sauropod*'s engines are started, Captain," Iggy reported.

"And I'm sending out a greetings message to the *Lightning Bolt* already," said Gipsy, "so we can make contact as soon as possible."

"Excellent," said Teggs. "Good luck, everyone. Let's go!"

Hours stretched on and on as the *Sauropod* sped through the endless night and nothingness of deep space.

Teggs checked the radar every few minutes to make sure the *Lightning Bolt* hadn't disappeared.

Gipsy listened out for signals or messages coming from the ancient craft. So far there had been none.

Iggy kept the engines well-stoked with

steaming dung
and helped
Sprite and his
dimorphodon
at the controls.

"Just four
hours to go until we
pull level with the *Lightning
Bolt*," Iggy announced.

"I'll send yet another greetings
message," said Gipsy. "If someone *is*
steering that ship, they've got to hear us
soon . . ."

Suddenly – "ROARRR!
SNARRRL!!! SNAP!" The ferocious
growls and rumbles echoed around
the flight deck and the dimorphodon
screeched and clattered about in alarm.

Teggs jumped out of his control pit.
"What is *that*?"

"I'm not sure." Gipsy frantically fiddled
with her controls. "Maybe it was space
static."

Iggy shook his head. "Sounded more like something big and bad-tempered with a bellyache." He frowned. "And look – the *Lightning Bolt*'s changed course!"

Teggs saw he was right. "Follow that ship!" he ordered, and the dimorphodon flapped into action. "Gipsy, those snarls – could they have been a reply to your greetings message in some strange language?"

"It's like nothing I've ever heard before," she admitted. "But if there *are* aliens on board, who knows what they sound like."

"We're catching them up!" Iggy reported, and sure enough, Teggs could see the battered old *Lightning Bolt* just a small way ahead of them on the scanner.

"Fire dung torpedoes well ahead of them as a warning to stop," said Teggs.

"Launching torpedoes," Iggy reported – and seconds later, a big brown

explosion splattered into space on the
scanner. The *Lightning Bolt* tried to steer
past – but another stinky blast erupted
close by, and the old ship's hull was
sloshed in sizzling dung. Moments later,
the crumpled craft ground to a halt.

"Did it!" Iggy cheered.

Teggs ran to Gipsy's communicator.
"Attention, *Lightning Bolt*," he said. "We

are astrosaurs. Please identify yourselves."

There was no answer.

"At least they aren't snarling any more," said Gipsy quietly.

"Perhaps that sudden stop hurt whoever's on board," said Iggy.

"Or perhaps it's a trick," said Teggs. He tried again. "*Lightning Bolt*, please respond. If you do not, we will come on board and steer your vessel back to the Vegetarian Sector of Dinosaur Space."

Again, there was no reply.

Teggs turned to a small, bright dimorphodon named Dactil. "Dactil, I'm leaving you in charge."

"Ker-chup!" said Dactil proudly, hopping into the control pit.

"Sprite, Iggy, Gipsy – get your fight gear on." Teggs

clenched his fists. "We're going to take a shuttle to the *Lightning Bolt* – and we'd better be ready for anything!"

Minutes later, Gipsy had put on her combat suit, Iggy was wearing his trusty

stun-claws and Teggs was good to go in full battle-armour. The three friends found Sprite waiting for them on board

the shuttle. He was wearing weapon-wings and a beak-blaster and looked very cool. "Chirp!"

Teggs smiled at Iggy. "That's dimorphodon-speak for 'BLAST OFF!'"

The four astrosaurs held on tight as the shuttle shot away towards the tarnished tin hulk of the long-lost *Lightning Bolt*. Compared to the *Sauropod* it looked a real wreck. Sprite steered them alongside the old ship's launch bay and a docking tube bound the two ships together.

Cautiously, Teggs led the way to the *Lightning Bolt*'s launch-bay door. It opened stiffly with a long, protesting creak. "Stay close, guys," he whispered as a musty animal smell struck his nostrils. Squinting into the gloom, Teggs tensed himself for trouble.

And a split-second later, he found it.

"ROARRRR!" A snarling shriek rang out as the lights snapped on — to reveal a huge, sandy-yellow cat monster. Its body was crammed with meaty muscles, its heavy paws bristled with claws and its amber eyes were narrowed in hatred. But it was the creature's teeth that held Teggs transfixed: they curved down from its mouth like giant vampire fangs and looked sharp enough to chomp through steel.

"Look out!" yelled Teggs. "There's some sort of sabre-toothed tiger-monster on board!"

The killer cat pounced towards him, snarling and drooling. Thinking fast, the stegosaur turned and swung his electro-tipped tail like a baseball bat. *THWUMP – bzzzzzz*! Blue sparks crackled around the attacking animal as Teggs thwacked it into the wall. But a moment later the cat was up again, ready to slash Teggs's side with its terrifying claws.

Then Sprite
swooped
overhead, his
beak-blaster
spitting bright
blue laser bolts.
The big cat swiped
the air, distracted – and
Iggy let rip with his stun-claws, shocking
the sabre-tooth into submission.

"I'm going in," called Teggs. "That
thing might have been holding the crew
prisoner." He kicked open the next door
and advanced through a cold,
rusty corridor into a gloomy chamber.
A gigantic juddering generator
dominated the space, its battered bulk
half-buried beneath a spaghetti of wires
and cables.

"This must be the ship's power room,"
said Gipsy.

Iggy nodded. "All heat and light on
board comes from this rickety old thing."

He patted the generator and frowned. "Strange – the engines have been rigged to run on electricity instead of dung."

"I don't suppose one big cat makes enough poo to power a spaceship for three hundred years," said Teggs.

Sprite squeaked a warning as two more sabre-toothed cats burst into the power room from the doors opposite.

"Or even *three* big cats," said Teggs as the creatures growled and grunted and pawed the air. "Er, maybe we should get back to the shuttle."

The astrosaurs edged back towards the door they'd just come through – but then the first cat smashed through it, angrier than ever.

Gipsy's head-crest flushed bright blue with alarm. "We're trapped!"

Chapter Four

A VOICE FROM THE PAST

Teggs backed away towards the generator – then waggled his hands and blew a raspberry at the sabre-tooths. "Come on then, you miserable moggies!" he jeered. "See what a stegosaurus tastes like!"

Enraged, the three cats ignored the other astrosaurs and charged straight at Teggs. But at the last minute he dived clear! The cats couldn't stop in time and smashed into the old generator ...

KA-TZZZZZZ! All three were consumed in white sparks and their skeletons flashed through their fur like x-rays. The wires and cables started

smoking and the lights flickered off and on again. Finally, the felines fell and flopped to the ground in front of the smoking machine.

Iggy quickly checked the damaged generator. "Life support systems still work, but the engines are completely *kaput*," he said. "This ship's going nowhere – ever again."

"Nor are these sabre-tooths," said Gipsy grimly, crouched beside the giant cats. "They're dead! The shock must have killed them."

"Dead?" Teggs felt sad and shaken. "I . . . I didn't mean for that to happen." He felt the biggest cat's neck for a pulse, but all he found was a small gold disc burned into the skin. "Looks like some sort of name tag. This one's name was Fangal."

Gipsy checked the others. "This one was Kerr and this one Clawdio."

Sprite flapped down and perched beside Fangal – then cheeped as the

38

cat's chest began to rise and fall again.

"You're right, Sprite," said Teggs in amazement. "She's alive!"

Gipsy checked the other furry forms. "I don't believe it! Kerr and Clawdio have come back to life too."

"That's freaky," said Iggy. "It's like they just . . . switched themselves back on."

"They're still pretty weak," Teggs observed. "I wonder if this ship has a sick bay."

Iggy nodded. "If I remember the layout of these old Dungmasters, it should be on the next level up."

"Take our feline friends there and strap them in so they can't hurt us – or themselves," said Teggs. "Sprite, give him a helping wing. Gipsy, we have to get to the flight deck and find out who's been flying this crate. Then we'll try towing it back to Outpost Q."

Iggy and Sprite gingerly hauled away Fangal, while Gipsy walked with Teggs along corridors that smelled of dust and decay.

"Where d'you think those sabre-tooths came from, sir?" she asked.

"Maybe the Jurassic Explorers kept them as pets!" Teggs joked. But inside he was worried. Where *had* the mysterious cats come from? What was their secret?

The flight deck was gloomy, with only a few bulbs working in the rusty ceiling. There was cat fur everywhere. Teggs and Gipsy inspected the ancient controls.

"This looks like a life-sign scanner." Gipsy picked up a dusty grey box. "You know, for telling the captain how many crew are on board and where they all are, in case of emergency." She pressed a switch and the box's screen flickered. Two green dots showed in the middle.

"That must be us," said Teggs. Further down the scanner, two more green dots popped into life beside three red blobs. "Different life-types must show in different colours. The green blobs must be Iggy and Sprite, reptiles like us."

"Which means the red blobs are the cats." Gipsy spoke into her communicator. "Iggy, this is Gipsy – how are things?"

"Not too hairy," Iggy reported. "We've got all three of our friends strapped into medical couches, but the auto-doctor must be playing up. It says that the cats are fit and healthy – but over three hundred years old!"

Teggs frowned. "That's impossible."

"They certainly didn't attack like old-age pensioners!" Gipsy agreed.

"Keep an eye on them, Ig," said Teggs. "We'll try and find out more here."

"Look, Captain!" Gipsy sat down in front of a dusty computer with a camera built in. "A message recorder. All announcements sent by the *Lightning Bolt* were recorded here in sound and pictures." She pressed a few buttons. "Looks like the last entry was recorded 276 years ago . . ."

Teggs tingled with excitement. "Can you put it on the screen?"

Gipsy fiddled with some buttons and then she and Teggs jumped as the image of a dark-green flesh-eating dinosaur flashed up on the screen. Bands of fuzz and static could not hide the beast's huge teeth and claws – nor the deep wounds scoring its scaly cheek.

"A carnivore!" Gipsy flinched instinctively. "Then meat-eaters must've attacked the *Lightning Bolt*."

"Not necessarily," Teggs reassured her.

"Quite a few of the Jurassic Explorers were carnivores. In those days space wasn't split down the middle between veggies and meat-munchers as it is now. We worked together more." He leaned forward keenly. "This one looks like a dryptosaurus – a distant cousin of T. rex. Let's hear what he has to say."

Gipsy hit a switch and the image jerked into life. "*This is Deputy Leader*

Alson of Jurassic Exploration eleven-two-four-six-nine . . ." The creature's gruff growl filled the dusty old control room; it was hard to believe he'd spoken these words centuries ago. *"Attacked . . . giant animals with fangs . . . terrible weapons . . ."* Suddenly both sound and picture dissolved into a fuzzy blur.

Teggs groaned. "What's wrong?"

"Their last message was cut off by space static," Gipsy reminded him. "It's worn away the tape."

"They care about nothing but war," Alson went on anxiously. *"We're running, but our*

luck won't hold for ever . . ." More static
bit into the picture. *"Never stop chasing
us. Can't go back . . . We will never see
home . . ."*

Teggs gasped as he saw a big sabre-
toothed cat bound up behind Alson on
the screen – and then the picture cut to
blackness.

Gipsy held her stomach queasily. "The
tape has snapped. But I think that was
the end of the message in any case."

"So now we know what happened
all those years ago," Teggs murmured.
"Fangal and her friends hunted down
and killed the Jurassic Explorers with
terrible weapons – then learned how to
fly their ship and took it for themselves."

Gipsy gulped. "Alson said that all they
care about is war."

"We'd better warn Iggy and Sprite,"
said Teggs. "Those cats are smarter than
they seem." He checked the old ship's
gun turrets and torpedo banks, but they

were empty. "No sign of any terrible weapons. Perhaps they've been used up . . . or perhaps they've been hidden somewhere on board."

Suddenly, a loud chime burst from the *Lightning Bolt*'s old communicator. Gipsy frowned. "It's a message from Arx back on Outpost Q!"

"Put him through," Teggs commanded. "Captain, it's me." Arx stared out at his friends from the scanner, looking grave. "Jodril has just spotted something through the Megascope – an unknown ship, approaching you from deep space. It's ignoring all greeting calls and refuses to identify itself."

Teggs raised his eyebrows. "Could

it be the same flying saucer that the triceratops scout ship saw near Outpost Q?"

"Possibly, Captain," said Arx. "We just don't know. But right now it's heading straight for the *Lightning Bolt* – on a collision course!"

Chapter Five

BREAKOUT !

Back on Outpost Q, Arx saw the concern
on Teggs and Gipsy's faces and longed
to be with them. Being stuck trillions of
miles away in safety was very frustrating.

"We'd better get back to the *Sauropod*,"
Teggs said. "And take our prisoners
with us."

"Prisoners?" Arx's
horns perked up.
"What prisoners?"

"Are they sabre-
tooths?" asked Chief
Spotter Speck. He'd
been checking the
Megascope, but now

hurried over to the scanner to address Teggs himself. "I repeat, have you found sabre-toothed cats on board?"

"Yes, three of them," Teggs confirmed. "How did you know?"

Speck looked awkward. "Er – lucky guess."

"Very lucky," said Arx thoughtfully.

"You must bring them back here," Speck said. "Quickly!"

"That's just what we plan to do," Teggs assured him. "So long, Arx. Over and out."

With a worried nod, Speck turned and hurried back out of the Megascope room.

"Wait, Chief Spotter," Arx called, following him as far as the doorway. "There's an unknown ship approaching the *Lightning Bolt,* and—"

But Speck had stormed away down the steps and into the Star Chart Library, closing and locking the door behind him.

"I thought that room was closed for cleaning," said Arx.

"It's been out of bounds for weeks," Jodril agreed.

Arx glared at the locked-up library. "Just how *did* Speck know there were sabre-tooths on board the *Lightning Bolt* three hundred years after it vanished?"

Jodril shrugged helplessly. "Come on –
let's keep an eye on this unmarked ship,"
she said. "At the speed it's going, it should
reach your friends within the hour!"

In the *Lightning Bolt*'s sick bay, Sprite
was pecking at the auto-doctor's
controls while Iggy watched warily. The
sabre-tooths lay silent, strapped into
their couches as soft bleeps and bloops
measured their heart rates and energy
levels.

Iggy jumped as Teggs and Gipsy
bundled in, a little out of breath.

"How are the patients?" asked Teggs.
"Or should I say, how are the deadly
war-like maniacs?"

"It looks like they killed the Jurassic
Explorers and took their ship," Gipsy
explained.

"Well, they're getting stronger all
the time." Iggy shook his head. "I just

don't understand it. They've recovered completely from a shock that should've killed them. Now they're just sleeping peacefully."

"In that case, we'll leave the cats here and tow the *Lightning Bolt* back to Outpost Q with our space-magnets," said Teggs.

Iggy frowned. "Why the sudden rush?"

"Because an unknown ship is speeding our way," Gipsy told him. "It might be a hostile vessel. We'd better get ready to fight."

But even as Gipsy said the word, Fangal burst through the hefty safety straps that bound her to the couch and rolled off with a throaty snarl. She landed on her feet, jaws hanging wide to show off her colossal curving canines, and butted Teggs in the belly. He staggered back against the wall. Then Kerr and Clawdio bit through their own safety straps and pounced straight at Gipsy!

The hadrosaur dived to the floor and the big cats flew over her, hitting the ground running. They escaped through the open door and hurtled out of sight.

With a growl, Fangal turned and made for the open door too. Iggy dived forward in a flying tackle, but the sabre-tooth was too quick and he hit the floor with an "Oof!" Sprite raised his weapon-wings and fired stun-beams at Fangal, but the sabre-tooth shrugged off the gunfire and fled after her friends, almost trampling Gipsy as she went.

"I don't believe it," Iggy fumed, helping Gipsy to her feet. "Those creepy cats got away!"

"There's no way off this ship apart from our shuttle on Level Zero," said Teggs, rubbing his stomach. "I guess we can leave the sabre-tooths to roam free until we get to Outpost Q, then call for reinforcements from the DSS."

"But what if Fangal and her mates are running to our shuttle now?" said Iggy. "They could be setting a trap for us – or stealing it for themselves."

"We found a life-sign scanner on the flight deck," said Gipsy. "It shows different life-types in different colours. By following the red blobs we can see exactly where Fangal and her two sidekicks have gone."

She switched it on and a diagram of the *Lightning Bolt's* layout glowed into life. Four green dots appeared first, huddled close together – the astrosaurs in the sick bay. Three red blips showed the sabre-tooths moving quickly through the ship, all the way to the top, where they finally stopped.

"There," said Teggs. "Safely out of the way on the top floor."

"That's where the old crew bedrooms would be," said Iggy.

"Phew," said Gipsy. "I guess they can't do much harm up there . . ."

But then another red blob appeared on the life-sign scanner. POP! And another, and another, popping up like the screen had a bad case of measles. POP-POP-POP-POP! More and more and more . . .

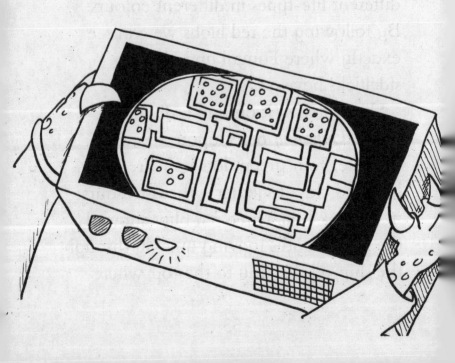

"Urp!" squeaked Sprite fearfully.

Teggs frowned. "Gipsy, is the scanner faulty?"

"No. I only wish it was." As the number of red blobs topped thirty she looked gravely at her friends. "Do you remember what happened after the sabre-tooths hit the generator and we thought they were dead?"

Iggy nodded. "It was like their bodies suddenly started up again. Like they'd woken from a deep, deep sleep."

"Exactly," Gipsy agreed. "And I think Fangal, Kerr and Clawdio just ran upstairs to wake a load of their sleeping friends!"

"They've switched on a whole army of sabre-tooths," breathed Teggs as more than fifty red blips began zooming back *down* through the ship towards the sick bay. "And now they're coming to get us!"

Chapter Six

FLIGHT INTO FEAR

Teggs bundled Iggy, Sprite and Gipsy out of the sick bay. Already he could hear the pound of furry feet on old, cold metal, and the scrape of killer claws. "Sprite, fly to the shuttle as fast as you can and start the engines," Teggs shouted.

"We'll catch you up as soon as possible."

"Come on," said Iggy as Sprite shot away. "If the sabre-tooths catch us, they'll tear us to pieces!"

The astrosaurs pelted along gloomy, run-down corridors as though raptors were biting at their tails. They took the steps down to Level Zero six at a time, hurtling round sharp corners and bouncing off the rusty walls as they sprinted for safety. But behind them, the wails and snarls of the caterwauling cats were growing louder and louder. Teggs risked a backward glance and gasped

HAVE A NICE DAY

as the army of sabre-tooths surged into sight round the corner, deadly teeth bared like big bone bananas . . .

"Faster!" Teggs urged Iggy and Gipsy. "Not much further now . . ."

The sound of engines rumbling and grumbling greeted them as they entered the launch bay. Iggy led the mad dash into the tube that led to the astrosaurs' shuttle, and in seconds all three friends had thrown themselves inside. But the rolling thunder of paws and claws was horribly close behind them.

"Shut the doors!" Teggs yelled, and Sprite bashed a button with his beak. The shuttle sealed itself with a satisfying *click* – just as a furry body smashed

60

against it, denting the bodywork.

"They don't give up easily, do they," Gipsy quavered.

"Nor do we," said Teggs, jumping back up. "Head for the *Sauropod*, Gipsy – that unmarked ship must be almost on top of us!"

Gipsy hit the dung-burner jets, and the shuttle tore away from the *Lightning Bolt*. Teggs couldn't wait to see the reassuring sight of his shiny egg-shaped ship through the windscreen.

But as the shuttle turned through space, the astrosaurs gasped to find a very different ship dead ahead of them, blocking their way. It was huge and imposing, bright red and boxy, glimmering in the starlight.

"The unmarked ship making for the *Lightning Bolt*," Teggs murmured. "It's arrived."

"But who's on board?" said Iggy. "And what do they want?"

"Eeep!" said Sprite, hiding his eyes with both wings.

"This is Captain Teggs calling the *Sauropod.*" Teggs spoke into his communicator. "Dactil, this is Shuttle Delta – come in, please." A harsh crackle of static came back in answer. "Dactil? Please respond!"

"That weird ship must be blocking our signals," groaned Iggy.

Gipsy's head-crest turned so blue it dazzled. "Or else it completely destroyed the *Sauropod* while we were trying to escape!"

Then a quiet hiss started up in the shuttle. "What's that?" Teggs turned round – and to his horror saw the tip of a claw poking through a tiny hole in the shuttle doors. "I don't believe it. There's a sabre-tooth clinging on out there!"

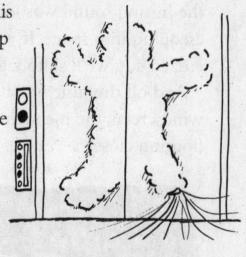

"It must be Fangal." Gipsy boggled. "But there's no air in space. She can't survive out here."

"Has anyone told *her* that?" cried Iggy as, with a sharp scratching noise, another claw popped into sight. Sprite pecked the claws with his beak, trying to weaken her hold. But an increased thumping and scraping started up on the other side of the door as Fangal tore at the metal all the harder.

"She's puncturing the doors," groaned Teggs: the holes were growing bigger and the hissing sound was louder. "Our air is escaping into space. If we don't stop that crazed cat, we'll suffocate!"

And all the time, through the shuttle windscreen, the menacing red ship was floating closer . . . *closer* . . .

★ ★ ★

Back at Outpost Q, Arx was squinting through the Megascope. The sinister dark red ship was blotting out his view of the *Sauropod,* and the *Lightning Bolt* was hiding the shuttle. Arx had tried calling both Dactil and his captain, but got nothing but static.

"Whatever the threat, they can handle it," he told himself, his horns drooping sadly. "I hope!"

"Arx!" Jodril came thumping into the room. She looked as worried and glum as he felt. "I've just come from the Data Room. I was searching for any other sightings of that approaching ship – but I stumbled on something else." She stretched out her long neck until her head was down by Arx's ear.

"Guess what. Speck *did* spot the flying saucer picked up by that triceratops scout ship. He logged the sighting himself."

Arx gasped. "Are you sure?"

"Positive," said Jodril. "He was on watch at the time."

"Then why didn't he tell anyone?" wondered Arx. "What *is* this mysterious saucer? Where did it come from?"

"I don't know," said Jodril. "But judging by its speed and direction, I think it came right here – a couple of weeks ago!"

"To Outpost Q?" Arx felt his bones tingle. "Speck has been lying to us. Where is he now?"

"Still in the Star Chart Library," said Jodril.

Arx called Security Chief Alass on his wrist-communicator. "Arx to Alass. Meet me at the Star Chart Library as soon as you can."

"Something to do at last!" the
ankylosaur boomed. "See you in a
minute, sir."

Jodril followed
Arx, and they
both found
Alass waiting
outside the
locked library
door. Arx
banged on it
with his horns.

"Open up, Speck," he called. "You've
got a lot of explaining to do." When
there was no reply, he turned to Alass.
"I'll charge the door, you whack it with
your tail. Ready?"

Alass nodded hopefully. "One . . .
two . . ."

"Three!" Arx head-butted the door just
as Alass smashed it with her bony club of
a tail. The door groaned open to reveal
only blackness on the other side.

"Speck?" Arx called, venturing into the darkness with Alass.

Then the ankylosaur screamed. Arx turned and glimpsed something huge and dark swooping down towards him.

Then he saw nothing at all . . .

Chapter Seven

FROM DANGER TO WHERE . . . ?

On board Shuttle Delta, Teggs was
desperately trying to block the holes in
the door. But it was no good – Fangal's
claws had left the shuttle's sides with
more perforations than a swamp-teabag.

Iggy was choking for breath. "It's no
good, Captain!"

"We've lost
too much air
already," Gipsy
groaned.

"No!" Teggs
felt his head start
to spin. "It can't
end like this!"

"Eeep." Sprite pointed through the windscreen to the red ship. A huge hatch was opening in its front like a mouth. As the shuttle drifted inside, the hatchway closed again.

This ship has taken us into its loading bay, Teggs realized. *Where there's air!* He took a deep, thankful breath as his head stopped spinning – but then he frowned.

Who was on board this vessel? Had they meant to save the astrosaurs – or were their motives more sinister?

Fangal roared, still clawing furiously at the shuttle's mangled doors. "No, you don't!" cried Teggs. "Damaging DSS property is a serious offence!" He lowered his armoured head and charged at the doors, smashing them open with such force that they fell off! Then he jumped on top of them, squashing the big cat underneath with all eight tons of his enormous bulk. She struggled, hissing and snarling,

and Teggs
felt like a surfer trying
to ride the wildest wave ever.

"Guys," he called back into the shuttle.
"Wake up, quickly. I don't know where
we are, but I can't hold Fangal for long."
The sabre-tooth snarled and grunted,
almost as if trying to speak. "If we stick
around here, this wildcat will whip our
butts, big time!"

Still sporting his stun-claws, Iggy
staggered out of the shuttle and Gipsy
followed with Sprite in her arms.
The loading bay was bare and black.

A single red doorway stood open, the only exit.

"There's nowhere else to go," said Gipsy weakly. "We'll have to risk it."

Once his friends were through, Teggs leaped away and galloped after them into *another* loading bay, large and empty. He glanced behind him and saw Fangal crawling out from under the doors, completely unharmed. There seemed to be a desperate edge to her roaring now . . .

The red bay door slammed shut, trapping her outside – for the time being at least. But then a noise behind them made the astrosaurs turn . . .

Teggs gulped when he saw that six towering carnivores had entered the second loading bay. They had big teeth. Their claws were as long as garden shears and ten times as sharp.

"Talk about out of the frying pan and into the fire." Iggy groaned. "This ship must belong to meat-eaters."

"Erp," Sprite agreed.

"Dryptosaurus by the look of them," said Gipsy.

Teggs nodded. "Like Alson, the Jurassic Explorer."

"Well, well," hissed the biggest dryptosaurus, tapping its terrible claws together. "Plant-eaters! What a stroke of

luck – when we're so hungry . . ."

Slowly, the drooling monsters began to close in. Teggs waved his armoured tail in warning and his crew braced themselves for combat . . .

But then the biggest carnivore bowed.

"Hello. My name's Wettus. This is Mrs Wettus, and these are our four children, Wet, Witt, Wutt and Wotnot."

"Cooeee!" The family waved shyly.

"Er . . . I'm Teggs," said Teggs. "This is Iggy, Gipsy and Sprite."

"Nice to meet you. Even nicer to *vegetable* you!" Wettus gave a hopeful smile. "Got any yummy plants on you then, my leaf-noshing friends? Any fresh ferns? Any carrots at all?"

"Am I going space crazy?" Iggy scratched his head. "I mean, you *are* meat-eaters, right?"

"Most dryptosaurus are," Wettus agreed, "but my family and I *hate* meat! We much prefer veggie food, just as my great-great-great-great-granddad Alson did."

"Alson?" Gipsy gasped. "As in, Alson the Deputy Leader of the *Lightning Bolt*?"

"That's him!" said Wettus cheerily. "Alson loved noshing plants – which is why he loved sharing a ship with veggie explorers."

"*Do* you have any food? It's been a very long journey." Mrs Wettus gestured round at the empty loading bay. "As you can see, our supplies have all gone."

"We've had to make a single bean last all six of us for a week!" young Wet complained.

Teggs could hardly believe what he was hearing – but the dryptosaurus seemed sincere. "Our ship, the *Sauropod*, has loads of food," he said. "Do you know where it's gone?"

"Oh, it's just outside," said Wettus brightly. "I'm afraid our communicator's on the blink. It's jamming local frequencies so we can't send or receive messages."

"And neither can any other craft in the area," Gipsy realized. "Dactil must be super-worried."

"You must let us fix the fault," said Iggy as a familiar banging and scratching started up from behind the storehouse doors. "Before that sabre-tooth gets through."

"Sabre-tooth?" said Wettus nervously. "That's a fanged animal, isn't it? Must be what my granddad Alson was talking about in the *Lightning Bolt*'s last message."

"We think so," said Teggs.

"There are loads of them on board that old crate," said Iggy.

But then the scratching stopped – and a sad whining and whimpering started up.

Gipsy frowned. "What's wrong with her all of a sudden?"

"It sounds like she's crying," said Wotnot. "Why?"

"I don't know," said Teggs. "This mystery keeps getting deeper. But first things first – we must fix your communicator and let Dactil know we're OK." He turned to Wettus. "Take us to your flight deck – and on the way you can tell us what you're all doing here."

"We're searching space for our long-lost great-great-great-great-grandfather's ship, of course!" Wettus and his family scuttled quickly through their bare and gloomy craft. "Tyrannosaurs mocked us because of our plant-munching ways. They drove us from our home on Bloodcrunch Four with their jibes and jokes."

"But no one laughed at Alson," said Wutt, "because he was a famous Jurassic Explorer."

"So now *we're* explorers too!" cheered Wotnot.

"Very hungry ones," grumbled Witt.

"If we can only find the fanged beasts' terrible weapons that Alson spoke of, we can take them to our ruler, King Drypto," said Wettus.

Mrs Wettus nodded. "He'll reward us well and then no one will laugh at us any more."

"Well, we didn't see any weapons on board that ship," Teggs told her. "And anyway – isn't there enough fighting between carnivores and plant-eaters as it is?"

Wettus shrugged. "I suppose so . . ." He led the way into a roomy flight deck, as bare and dark as the rest of the ship.

Iggy rushed to the communicator and soon found the fault. "There's fluff in the main sprockets."

Sprite used his delicate beak to pull the fluff clear, and at once an angry cheeping echoed from the black ship's speakers.

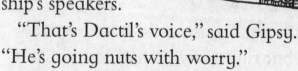

"That's Dactil's voice," said Gipsy. "He's going nuts with worry."

"Dactil, this is your captain," said Teggs quickly. "We're all fine. Please point our space-magnets at the *Lightning Bolt* and tow it back to Outpost Q. We'll follow on in this spaceship. Don't worry, it's friendly – I hope." He glanced back at Wettus, who was smiling and nodding and pointing to his tum. "Oh, yes," Teggs added. "Can you send over some fresh plant stew? You'll have to use Loading Bay Two because we've got a crying sabre-toothed cat in Bay One."

For a few moments, Dactil was speechless. "Chi-chi," he said at last.

"You're absolutely right," Gipsy agreed. "It *has* been one of those days!"

The moment the *Sauropod*'s food parcel arrived in Loading Bay Two, Wettus and his family tore it open and gorged on grass and stew.

Normally, Teggs would have joined them, but right now he had lost his appetite.

Arx and Alass weren't answering his calls. Outpost Q was as silent as space.

While Sprite kept trying to get

through, Teggs, Gipsy and Arx went to check on the sabre-tooth.

They didn't have to worry about getting lost on the dryptosaurus ship – they just followed the sound of Wettus and his family chomping and slobbering! Their merry chewing drowned out the mournful mewing of Fangal in Bay One, still on the other side of the door.

"She almost tore her way through the side of our shuttle," Gipsy remembered. "I wonder why she's so quiet now."

"Probably worn out," said Wettus, gulping down ferns.

"Alson?" came a gruff yowl.

Iggy blinked. "Who said that?"

"Is it you? It smells like you, Alson." The growl grew louder. "Let me in! It's Fangal!"

Teggs gasped. "I don't believe it. The sabre-tooth can talk dinosaur!"

"I'm Wettus – Alson was my great-great-great-great-grandfather." The dryptosaurus turned to the door excitedly. "Tell me about the terrible weapons he spoke of! Where are they?"

"Most are still on board the *Lightning Bolt*," Fangal said sadly. "But one is here on your ship."

Teggs felt prickles go down his tail. "Of course," he breathed. "The sabre-tooths are indestructible. They don't need air. They never age, and they can shred metal and flesh as though it was paper." He glared at Wettus. "*There* are your terrible weapons – the cats themselves!"

Chapter Eight

HIDDEN MENACE

"Please, let me in, offspring of Alson!" Fangal said through the door. "I will do no harm."

Wettus gulped. "Can we trust her?"

"Yes." Gipsy nodded slowly. "Somehow, I just know she's telling the truth."

"Well, you're the expert in communicating," said Teggs. "All right, Iggy – open the door."

Keeping his stun-claws at the ready, Iggy hit the red button beside the door to Loading Bay One. It slid open – and Fangal came inside.

Ignoring the astrosaurs, she bowed down
to Wettus.

"Golly!" said Wettus, wiping stew from
his lips. "Er . . . whatever are you doing?"

"Your ancestor Alson was a dear friend
of mine," Fangal purred. "I bow to you
in honour of his memory."

"Wait a sec," said Teggs. "Alson was
your *friend*? But we thought you attacked
the *Lightning Bolt*."

"Not us." Fangal shook her shaggy

head. "We sabre-tooths were created by war-like aliens called the Battalasks. They bred us to be an army of perfect killers." She sighed. "But at heart we are peaceful animals. We don't want to be used as weapons."

"How did you end up with the Jurassic Explorers?" asked Gipsy.

"The *Lightning Bolt* passed the battle-planet where we were being trained. The Explorers found us and helped us escape." Fangal growled as if at a bad memory. "The Battalasks were angry. They chased the Explorers through space, trying to recapture us. And they have kept hunting for us ever since."

"These Battalasks," said Teggs.

"Would they have giant fangs?"

"Fangs down to their feet," the sabre-tooth agreed. "Far bigger than my own."

"Then that makes sense of Alson's garbled message," Teggs realized. "It was the *Battalasks* attacking the *Lightning Bolt*, trying to get the sabre-tooths – who were already on board!"

Fangal nodded. "The Explorers couldn't risk returning to Dinosaur Space, in case the Battalasks followed them and waged war against your kind."

"Why didn't you just tell us all this when we came on board?" asked Iggy. "Why did you pretend to be savage animals and attack us?"

"We wanted to scare you away,"

Fangal admitted. "If you took us into Dinosaur Space, the Battalasks might follow, and Alson's worst fears would come true." She purred at Wettus. "Alson was my friend. He died peacefully of old age two hundred years ago, and never stopped caring for us sabre-tooths. He even wired the ship to run on electricity instead of dung, since we do not produce it."

"You never poo?" Iggy marvelled.

"After hearing *that* story, I need to go right now!" said Wotnot, and his brothers chased after him to the ship's toilet.

"Just think," said Gipsy. "If it wasn't for the Megascope, we would never have spotted the *Lightning Bolt,* and Fangal and her friends would have simply passed us by."

"Are my fellow sabre-tooths still safe on board the *Lightning Bolt*?" Fangal asked eagerly.

"Yes," Teggs confirmed. "But you will

all have to come into Dinosaur Space now. With the *Lightning Bolt*'s power down there's nowhere else you can go."

"But don't worry," Gipsy added. "The DSS will help you."

Teggs smiled to see ahead of them a familiar cube with a huge tube sticking out of it. "And there's Outpost Q. We should arrive within the hour!"

Sure enough, fifty-five minutes later,
Teggs, Iggy, Gipsy and Sprite – as well
as Wettus and Fangal – were squeezed
into the *Sauropod*'s Shuttle Delta on their
way to Outpost Q. Iggy had fixed the
broken doors so they were airtight once
again.

"Chief Spotter Speck will get a shock
when he sees who we've brought with
us," remarked Gipsy as Sprite steered
them closer.

"It would be nice to let him know
in advance," said Teggs, "but there's
still no one answering Outpost Q's

communicator. I hope Arx and Alass are all right." He consoled himself with the thought that the three shuttles he'd left defending the outpost were still on patrol as normal. Their dimorphodon crews had reported no spaceship sightings – nothing out of the ordinary at all.

Once Sprite had safely landed Shuttle Delta, Teggs led his party into the outpost. The cavernous corridors were deserted.

"Where is everyone?" wondered Gipsy. "Why aren't the ankylosaurs on guard duty?"

Suddenly, a distant, muffled chorus of cries and caterwauls started up. "That's coming from the Data Room," said Teggs. He ran up to the door, peered through the small window beside it – and got a shock. "Er . . .

the Data Room seems to be doubling as the Room Where Staff Are Bound and Gagged!"

The rest of Teggs's group crowded round to see. There were over a dozen apatosaurus lying inside, all tied up with thick ropes and calling out through the towels and tablecloths muzzling their jaws. Their long necks were intertwined in a scaly tangle, and they looked very sorry for themselves.

"How did this happen?" Teggs cried. "No wonder no one was answering my calls. We must get these poor dinosaurs out." The door was locked, and he was about to try to smash it down when Fangal pressed a heavy paw against his side.

"Wait," she growled. "Someone is coming."

Teggs turned as Chief Spotter Speck burst into sight at the end of the corridor. "Help!" Speck yelled. "Arx and Alass and all your crew are in danger in the Star Chart Library. Is that Fangal? You must bring her quickly . . ." He tailed off at the sight of Wettus. "Hang on, that's a meat-eater! Ugh! What's it doing here?"

"I'm a *he*, thank you very much!" Wettus shot back crossly. "I'm a veggie and related to one of the Jurassic Explorers, so there."

"Then you'd better come too," said Speck, ducking out of sight.

"Wait!" Teggs cried, galloping after him. "Your staff have been locked up – we must get them out. And what do you mean, my crew are in danger?"

"Hang on, Captain," said Gipsy, racing after him with Sprite at her side. "How did Speck know Fangal's name?"

"And how come he's free when his workers are all tied up?" Iggy added, following on with Fangal while poor wheezing Wettus lagged behind.

But Teggs was so worried about Arx and his team that he ran recklessly into the Star Chart Library, smashing open the door with a swipe of his spiky tail. He had no real plan – which was just as well.

Because nothing could ever have prepared him for the sight inside.

Arx, Alass and her ankylosaurs lay tied
up and gagged just like the victims in the
Data Room, their wrist-communicators
smashed. Jodril lay helplessly beside
them while Speck stood sorrowfully in
the corner. And hanging upside down
from the high ceiling were twelve of

the biggest, nastiest-looking monsters
Teggs had ever seen. They had huge
leathery wings like giant pterosaurs,
but their faces were bat-like, wrinkled
with folds of flesh. Strange-looking
headsets covered their big round ears,
and stupendous pointed teeth poked out

of their mouths like ivory stalactites, so long that they threatened to pierce the monsters' three hairy feet.

Fangal bounded in behind Teggs – and then skidded to a halt. "Oh, no," she whispered, shaking with horror. "The Battalasks . . . they've found me!"

Gipsy's head-crest turned electric blue. "*Those* are the things that created you?"

"Yes, puny dinosaurs," hissed the largest Battalask, swooping to the ground.

"I am Major Terrorkon. I assume the rest of the sabre-tooths are still on board the *Lightning Bolt*. Thank you for delivering them back to their rightful owner. Your reward will be a terrible death!"

Chapter Nine

BATTLING BATTALASKS

"There's no need to reward us, prune-
face," said Teggs coolly. "Just explain how
you got into this outpost. My shuttle
crew told me no spaceships had come
this way."

"Fool," hissed Terrorkon. "We came
well before you arrived. Our ship is
parked in secret beneath this space
station. We have been hiding here all
along."

"That vessel the triceratops ship
spotted in the area . . ." Teggs groaned,
and the bound-and-gagged Arx nodded
sadly. "It was you and your ugly friends
arriving."

Terrorkon wrenched the communicator from Teggs's wrist, and took Iggy's and Gipsy's too. "We captured your crew one by one, and stopped them from warning you – like so." He crushed the bracelets in his toothy mouth.

Just then, Wettus lumbered in – and at the sight of the Battalasks he shrieked at the top of his lungs.

The monsters flapped down from their perches, filling the air as they flew around. One of them knocked Wettus over with a mighty wing – *whack!* – and he fell silent.

Taking advantage of the distraction, Fangal lunged at Terrorkon with her wicked claws. But two more Battalasks wrapped their wings around her, trapping her and squashing her inside.

"Don't hurt her," Gipsy implored.

"She cannot be hurt," Terrorkon whispered. "That is why she and her kind are such a prize." He turned to Teggs. "Really I should thank you for fetching Fangal for me, Captain. I was expecting to have to go myself, but you have saved me a tedious errand."

As the other creatures returned to their clawholds on the ceiling, Teggs realized he couldn't see Sprite anywhere. *Perhaps he flapped outside in the confusion*, he thought. *Perhaps he'll warn the* Sauropod *and call in a DSS attack fleet . . .*

But would it come in time?

"I don't understand." Iggy helped up Wettus and glared at Speck. "How could you let these things hide here?"

Speck wrung his hands and feet miserably. "I had no choice. I . . . owed them my help."

"Yes, you did," Terrorkon hissed. "We were searching for the sabre-tooths in deep space when we chanced upon Speck here, trying to build his telescope. We agreed to make it a million times better with Battalask technology . . ."

"But only so *you* could use it to hunt for the sabre-tooths," Gipsy realized.

"They . . . they said they would leave peacefully as soon as they'd found Fangal." Speck sighed. "At the time, hiding them here seemed a small price to pay for the best telescope in the galaxy."

"And you were happy to take all the credit for yourself," sneered Iggy.

"Enough of this noisy talking," hissed Terrorkon. "I have spent the last three hundred years chasing the sabre-tooths. All the other Battalasks gave up on them a century ago, building boring battle-robots instead. They thought me mad to keep searching." He smiled nastily, his giant fangs agleam. "But such a breathtaking army was well worth waiting for."

"Meeting you wasn't." Teggs pretended to yawn – and as he did so, out of the corner of

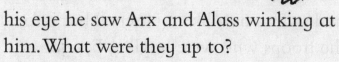

his eye he saw Arx and Alass winking at him. What were they up to?

Fangal wormed her head out from between the Battalasks' wings. "We will never fight for you. Never!"

"My Battalask brain-tools will change the way you think," rasped Terrorkon. "When I control you completely, I shall turn you on the rulers of Battalask and take charge of our empire myself!" His bat-like troops rustled their wings as if in applause. "Then I shall breed millions more indestructible sabre-tooths – and their first act will be to invade the

Jurassic Quadrant and turn the dinosaur empire into rubble!"

"Rubble?" Arx cried, whipping off his gag. "Rub*bish*!"

At the same time, Alass jumped up and whacked Terrorkon with her large club of a tail! He staggered in surprise and tried to take off – but Teggs hooked his tail round two of Terrorkon's hairy feet and swung him like a baseball bat into the troops who were holding Fangal within their wings. As they crashed to the floor, the big cat pounced free of their grip with a triumphant roar.

"Make a noise, everyone," Arx boomed. "Battalasks hate a racket!"

A horrendous hubbub started up as Wettus screeched, Fangal growled and Gipsy hooted at record-breaking volume. The Battalasks clutched their ears and flapped about like giant startled sparrows. Then Iggy started singing a very rude song about a diplodocus with

five legs – and the naughty words alone
were enough to make two of the bat-
aliens crash into each other.

"Arx!" Teggs beamed as the triceratops
punched a Battalask right in the fangs.
"How did you break free?"

"Chirrup!" Sprite flew out from behind
Jodril with ropes in his beak and flapped
over to untie some ankylosaurs.

Gipsy grinned. "Way to go, Sprite!"

"Yeah, thanks, little guy!" Jodril
jumped to her enormous feet and joined
the fray. "I've no idea what's going on or

where the veggie meat-eater came from, but I do love a good noisy knees-up!" And, wailing like an opera singer, she kneed Terrorkon in the face!

Iggy helped Arx wrestle another Battalask to the floor. "How did you guess that these things hated noise?"

Arx shrugged. "They hang out in libraries, speak in whispers and wear funny headgear to protect their ears."

"And when Wettus screamed, it sent them scattering," Teggs added, dodging a near-fatal fang bite. "I guess that explains why they need the sabre-tooths to fight for them even though they're scary enough themselves – war is just too noisy for them!"

But the Battalasks were still fearsomely strong. And now the astrosaurs and their friends had lost the element of surprise, the aliens were fighting back. Terrorkon swept Wettus aside with one wing and smashed Alass with a three-footed mega-kick. Winded, she hurtled into her ankylosaur troops like a bowling ball hitting skittles. Iggy found himself thrown into Jodril, who fell against Speck – the two apatosaurus almost squashed

Teggs, Arx and Gipsy as they fell. Sprite pecked furiously at the stubborn knot holding the last ankylosaurs – only to be swatted aside by a Battalask's fangs. He flew helplessly into Fangal's left eye and bowled the big cat over.

"Attention, Battalask troopers," Terrorkon whispered eerily. "We must leave for our spaceship at once."

"Hey!" said Iggy. "We've got them on the run. They're retreating."

"Battalasks never retreat," Terrorkon retorted. "Once inside our ship, we will take off and destroy your various spacecraft. Then we will blow Outpost Q to bits. And *then* we shall collect the unkillable Fangal from the debris, lock her up with her friends and take the whole lot of them back to our war-world to fight." He swept away, chuckling to himself. "Goodbye, fools. You are free to make as much noise as you like . . . as you *die!*"

Chapter Ten

SOUND AND FURY

"We can't just let the Battalasks get away," Iggy protested.

"How can we stop them?" groaned Jodril.

Fangal shook her huge head. "With the *Lightning Bolt*'s engines not working, my fellow sabre-tooths cannot escape."

"And my poor family can't steer my ship without me," said Wettus. "They'll be obliterated."

"So will the *Sauropod*," said Teggs. "We must warn everyone."

"We can't," said Speck. "Terrorkon destroyed the outpost's communicators, just as he smashed your own."

"The Megascope room," cried Arx, struggling out from under Speck's long yellow tail. "We must all go there quickly. I might just have a plan . . ."

He charged away, and Teggs led the ragtag group of unlikely allies after him, into the outpost's huge control room. Through the windows he saw the *Sauropod* and its shuttles, the *Lightning Bolt* and Wettus's ship hanging silently in space, blissfully unaware of the approaching danger.

"Arx, will you tell us your plan?" asked Teggs. "We're all ears."

"And so are the Battalasks," said Arx, studying the Megascope closely. "Sound is their weakness – and if I can rewire these circuits, perhaps we can use it against them."

Alass and her guards looked blank. "Huh?" they chorused.

"The Megascope magnifies light from space, and uses it to send an image into this room," Arx explained. "But if I can fix the Megascope so that it turns light waves into *sound* waves – and then reverse the settings – it should magnify *noise* from in here and send it out into space at supersonic volume . . ."

"Straight into the Battalask ship!" Jodril gasped in admiration. "That's brilliant."

Iggy grinned. "The perfect anti-Battalask weapon."

"You'll ruin my beautiful Megascope!" Speck wailed.

Teggs glowered at him. "What does that matter with so many lives at stake?"

"I suppose so." Speck sighed. "It's a very clever plan, Arx. But I fear it will take too long to make the changes –

the Battalask ship will pop up at any moment."

"Then we'd better get started." Arx's big paws were a blur as he started twisting wires and plugging them into different sockets.

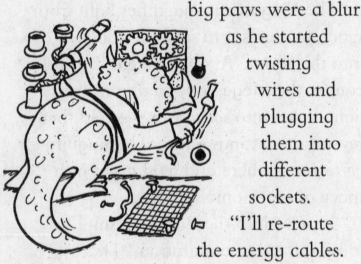

"I'll re-route the energy cables. Speck – start turning the light receivers into sound broadcasters. Jodril, change the focus on the galactic lens to short-range transmission . . ."

Alass watched as Jodril and Speck got to work. "I hope they know what they're doing."

"I hope they know how to do it in ten seconds flat." Gipsy's head-crest, already dazzling blue, was edging towards neon brightness. "Because here come the Battalasks!"

A grey saucer-shaped spaceship came rising up into view through the outpost's large windows. Without warning or pity it blasted the *Sauropod* with death lasers, and a massive brown explosion splattered into space.

"They've hit our dung torpedoes!" shouted Alass.

"Now Dactil can't defend the ship." Iggy stared helplessly. "The *Sauropod*'s a sitting duck!"

"How much longer, Arx?" Teggs demanded.

"We're going as fast as we can," the triceratops said calmly.

BWAMMMM! The Battalasks fired again and the dryptosaurus ship lurched and spun, leaking thick smoke.

Wettus covered his eyes. "Another direct hit like that and my family is doomed!"

Jodril stretched her long neck up to the Megascope's mid-section and pulled out a thick lens with her teeth. "Getting there," she mumbled.

Speck nodded, jabbing a circuit with a screwdriver. "But we need more time!"

"Time's up," said Gipsy as the Battalask ship started turning to face them.

"Maybe not," said Fangal, her eyes widening. "Look!"

Teggs stared – and a slow smile of disbelief spread over his face as a stream of sabre-tooths poured out of the *Lightning Bolt*'s launch bay! Led by Kerr and Clawdio, more than fifty of the big cats swam through the vacuum of space and attacked the Battalask ship. They tore chunks from its hull with their big claws and punctured its lasers with their deadly teeth.

"The Battalasks bred the sabre-tooths for war," said Teggs. "And now the sabre-tooths have declared war on *them*!"

"Come on, come on . . ." Arx hit some buttons on the Megascope and the lights on its side turned from green to red. "If the cats can keep them distracted a little longer . . ."

"Look!" Alass yelled. "The Battalasks are coming out to fight the sabre-tooths!"

Teggs stared, riveted with wonder. Almost invisible against the darkness of space in their black, billowing spacesuits,

Battalask warriors were flitting out of the holes torn in their ship. Furious fighting broke out with the big cats.

Fangal watched the conflict, shiny-eyed. "Battle, brothers and sisters!" she urged them. "Battle for your lives!"

Jodril slotted another lens into place, Speck inserted his circuits, and Arx threw a switch that set the whole Megascope vibrating with unearthly energy.

"We have power!" Arx yelled. "No time for proper tests. Make a noise, everybody. Make all the noise you can and we'll blast it at the Battalasks!"

"You heard Arx!" Teggs started hollering and honking and banging his tail against the floor. "Let's raise the roof!"

The ankylosaur guards jumped up and down and crashed about. Iggy wailed and screeched. Wettus and Fangal roared in harmony, and Sprite surprised everyone with an ear-splitting squawk

that almost blasted Teggs's ears off!

"It's working!" Arx shouted excitedly.

The Battalask ship had started to shake. Terrorkon's warriors clutched their space helmets, trying to block their ears. As if sensing their work was done, Clawdio, Kerr and the other sabre-tooths pushed away from the hull, swimming through space back towards the *Lightning Bolt*.

"Keep going, everyone," Teggs commanded. "Louder! LOUDER!"

Iggy punched a hole through the bottom of a bin and used it like a megaphone to amplify his yells. Gipsy let out a colossal hoot that almost broke every window in the place. Teggs blew a really loud raspberry, which made Jodril guffaw at amazing volume.

"The sonic vibrations are battering the Battalask ship," Speck said. "If they don't retreat soon, it will rattle itself apart!"

"You heard Terrorkon," Teggs said grimly. "Battalasks never retreat . . ."

And as the noise of the astrosaurs and their allies reached mega-mad levels, the alien warcraft broke into pieces! Explosion followed explosion in a crimson rush of flaming fragments. Outpost Q rocked and shuddered, and the Megascope swayed like a ship's mast in the stormiest sea.

But when the aftershocks of the blasts had faded, both were still intact.

"We did it," Gipsy breathed in the sudden silence.

A small tear dripped from Fangal's eye. "My people are free at last."

"And our families and crews are safe," said Teggs. "Woo-hoo!" He cheered, and everyone joined in. Alass and her ankylosaurs lifted Arx onto their shoulders and swept him around the room. Even Speck did a small victory dance with Jodril, accidentally squashing two control panels in the process!

"Well, Wettus," said Teggs, once the celebrations had calmed down. "You were hoping to stop other carnivores laughing at your veggie tastes by bringing them terrible weapons. Is that still your plan?"

"I would never dream of telling King Drypto about Fangal and the sabre-tooths," Wettus declared. "My great-great-great-great-granddad wanted to watch out for them, and now, so do I."

"Thank you." Fangal licked his cheek fondly. "If only we could find a nice quiet planet and all settle down together."

"Ooooh, yes," Wettus agreed. "A place where we could really belong."

"You can," said Speck. "I have already spotted hundreds of distant, deserted planets through the Megascope – most of them well off the beaten space track."

Arx beamed. "One of them will be perfect for you, I'm sure."

"Will there be lots of lovely plants growing there?" Wettus was licking his lips. "Will there?"

"We'll make sure of it," Teggs promised with a grin. "Then you can invite us all round for tea as soon as you're settled!"

"I'll untie the other apatosaurus and we'll start the search together," Jodril told Fangal. "Right, Chief Spotter?"

"Of course," said Speck. "It's the least I can do after being so foolish. I'll rebuild the Megascope myself – and I'll never take help from evil aliens again."

"Make sure you don't!" said Arx.

Teggs nodded, smiling fondly at his wonderful spaceship through the window. The three shuttles had parked outside, and dimorphodon in spacesuits were already repairing the Battalasks' damage.

"We'd better get back to Dactil and tell him everything's fine," said Iggy.

"Eep," Sprite agreed.

"And then," said Gipsy, "once we've sent Wettus and Fangal and their families on their way . . ."

"We can set off on another adventure," said Arx.

"Sounds like a plan to me!" Teggs grinned. "I may not have big, long fangs, but a new adventure is something I can ALWAYS get my teeth into!"

THE END

ASTRO PUZZLE TIME

THE SABRE-TOOTH SECRET
QUIZ Questions

1. What is the name of the legendary spaceship that belonged to the Jurassic Explorers?

2. What was the name of the sabre-tooths' leader?

3. What item of food have Wettus and his family had to survive on for a week?

4. Why did the Tyrannosaurs mock Wettus and his family?

5. What do the Battalasks really hate?

6. What is Iggy's very rude song about?

Answers:

6. A diplodocus with five legs.

5. Noise

4. Because of their plant-munching ways

3. A single bean

2. Fangal

1. Lightning Bolt